THE REAL STORY OF THE CREATION

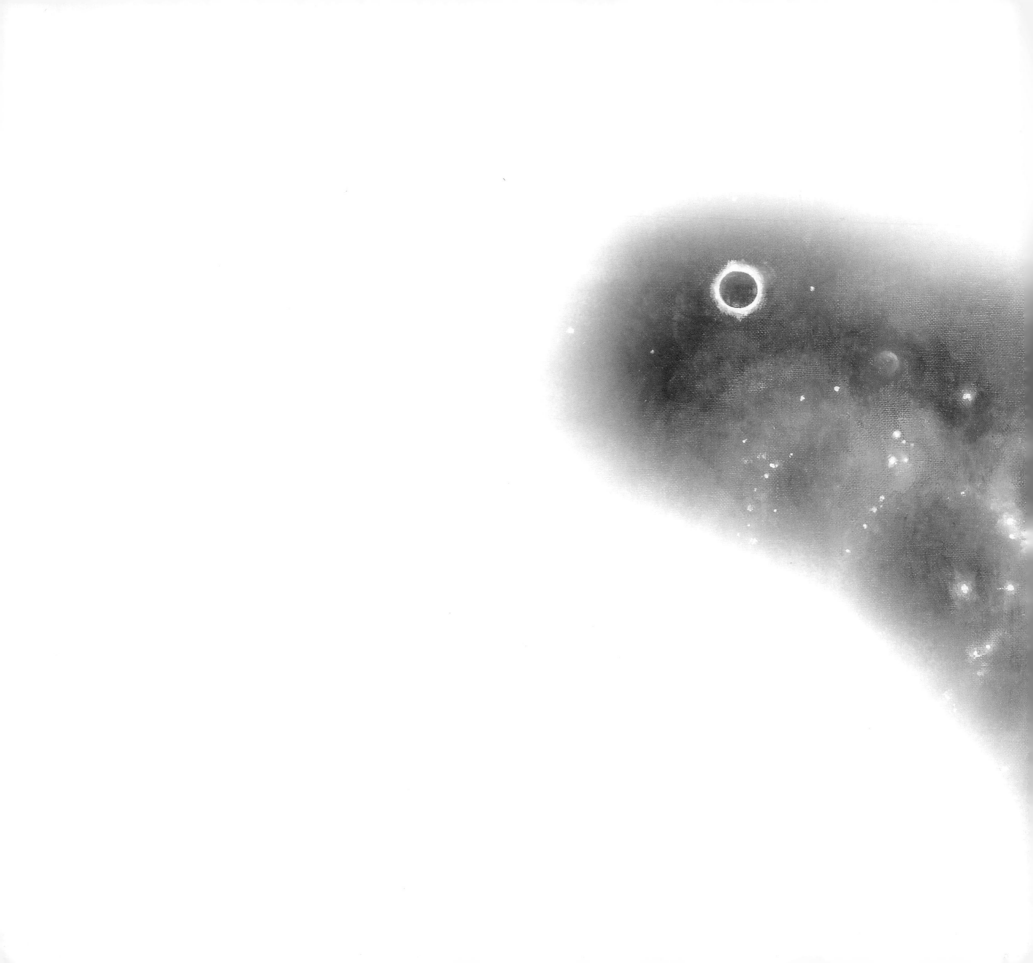

# THE REAL STORY OF
# THE CREATION

*by*

PAUL L. MAIER

*Illustrated by* Robert T. Barrett

CONCORDIA PUBLISHING HOUSE • SAINT LOUIS

Published by Concordia Publishing House
3558 S. Jefferson Avenue • St. Louis, MO 63118-3968
1-800-325-3040 • www.cph.org

Text copyright © 2007 by Paul L. Maier
Illustrations copyright © 2007 Concordia Publishing House

Manufactured in China.

1  2  3  4  5  6  7  8  9  10          16  15  14  13  12  11  10  09  08  07

## PROLOGUE

How did everything begin? The universe, planet Earth, or you yourself?

"Well, I came from my parents," you answer. That's right. But where did *they* come from?

"My grandparents," you reply.

Right again! But now let's keep going back to *their* parents and *their* grandparents—and so on, all the way back to the start of it all. How did life on earth begin? For that matter, how did the world itself and everything in it get here?

CHAPTER ONE

These are deep, important questions people have been asking for ages and ages, and some of their answers are amusing.

Mesopotamians living in the ancient Near East gave us the world's first civilization, but they believed that Marduk, a hero-god, killed a watery monster named Tiamat, cut her body in two, and the upper half became sky and the lower half earth.

The ancient Egyptians would have us believe that a sun god named Re sat on a hill of living slime near what is today Cairo, called out the names of various gods and goddesses, and—presto!—they appeared, along with the universe.

Now surely the Greeks were bright people and the Romans a powerful race, so we would expect them to know better than this. But no! They taught that Heaven married Earth and had gigantic offspring named Titans. The youngest one, Kronos, devoured his own children—except for Zeus, who hid out on the island of Crete. Zeus grew up and forced his father to spit out his brothers and sisters. They became the gods and goddesses of mythology.

Some people today believe there is no God and that all of us got here by luck or by accident. This is just as wrong as the ancient beliefs.

Now let's check out what really happened at the start of it all. …

CHAPTER TWO

*In the beginning God created the heavens and the earth. Genesis 1:1*

This is the very first sentence in the greatest book ever written. One opening verse in the Bible tells it all and gives us the whole story of Creation. God was the Creator—one God, not many—the divine Designer of all that is. He's not a male deity or a female goddess and He's not the same as Mother Nature. He's far greater than all that.

Some questions are probably swirling around in your head, and I'll bet here are some of them. …

*When did this happen?* At the start, of course—the very beginning—which is as far back as you can go. Don't try to figure out a year or century or millennium for this greatest of all events, because you can't. The concept of time itself began with the Creation.

*How was God able to do this?* Our God can do anything.

*What elements, materials, or ingredients did He use?* None at all. The word "created" in the Hebrew language of the Old Testament means to "make something from nothing."

*But that's impossible, isn't it?* For us, yes, of course! But with God, all things are possible.

*If He created heaven and earth, what about the planets and the rest of the universe?* We're coming to that. …

CHAPTER THREE

*The earth was formless and empty, darkness was over the surface of the deep. Genesis 1:2*

We now come to the details of how God brought all this off. He didn't wave His hand and announce, "Let everything come into existence—instantly!" Instead He created one thing at a time.

At first, everything seemed to be chaos in the cosmos! When the Book of Genesis tells us that the earth was "formless and empty," the Hebrew in which it was written uses the expression "tho-hu-wa-vo-hu," which means that the world was "one great big shapeless nothing."

As if that weren't enough, it was a dark nothing—no light by which to arrange things and bring order to the void. Had the universe remained this way, Creation would have been meaningless.

But "the Spirit of God hovered over the face of the waters," as the Bible says, and things changed.

CHAPTER FOUR

*And God said, "Let there be light," and there was light. Genesis 1:3*

Having created matter—the raw material of the universe—God then filled it with *energy;* energy in the form of light. Light has to be one of God's greatest inventions, a phenomenon most like Himself. Light fills our universe, much as God does. And so— in the distant future, when the Creator sent His Son to be a man—it's no accident that Jesus is called "the Light of the World."

Since darkness came before light, the Bible says that evening and morning were Day One of Creation. On another day God arranged that this light would shine from magnificent sources: the sun ("the greater light") by day, the moon ("the lesser light") and the stars by night.

Nothing shows off the majesty of our Creator better than to walk outside on a starry night and gaze overhead. Each star in the sky is as bright as the sun, but a vast distance further off, and most of them are much larger and brighter than our sun. Everything you can see—the moon, planets, meteors, stars, constellations, comets, and space itself— *all* of them were created by God, not only to provide magnificent beauty for us each night, but also to mark the seasons, years, and days.

Who but God could have arranged all this?

CHAPTER FIVE

*God said, "Let the water under the sky be gathered to one place, and let dry ground appear." Genesis 1:9*

After light and darkness were separated, the world was still without much shape or form. You'd never take a walk there because you'd sink down over your head into something like thick soup or lumpy pudding. If a farmer had a field like that, the first thing he'd do would be to drain it.

God did the very same thing—only on a cosmic scale! He separated water and land, letting the lower spots on the earth's crust remain wet and the higher spots dry out. Whole continents rose above the oceans, a sight so spectacular that God alone—the only witness—could appreciate it. Now there were beaches along the oceans, broad plains cut by rivers and streams, towering mountains and deep valleys, all of this a panorama of immense beauty.

Still, something was missing: everything was barren. There was no *life* around —no forests, no plants, no animals, no people—like pictures of the moon or Mars.

But the Creator also took care of that. *"Let the earth put forth vegetation,"* He commanded, and then the vast desert of the world came to life in the brilliant greens, browns, reds, yellows, and all the other colors we see in the plants and trees, wildflowers, shrubbery, vines, and foliage. This was our planet's first great spring!

CHAPTER SIX

*God created ... every living and moving [creature]. Genesis 1:21*

At last the world was now more like we imagine a lush paradise to be. Yet something was still missing. Other than the wind rustling in the trees, waves crashing on the beach, or a brook gurgling through the forest, there were no sounds! No birds were singing in the skies, no dogs barking behind houses (of course, no houses either!), and no animals of any kind. How about fishing? Sorry: there were no fish to be caught anywhere.

But the Lord who set the stage would also bring on the action. *"Let the waters bring forth swarms of living creatures,"* He directed. And now the seas were filled with wriggling fish, diving whales, jumping dolphins, crawling lobsters, and all the incredible marine life that dazzles us to this day. And that wasn't all. …

The God who created the skies filled them as well. He called the winged creatures into existence: birds of every kind, ranging from the tiny sparrow to the soaring eagle, each singing praises to their Creator in a different key.

Then it was the land's turn. God said, *"Let the earth bring forth living creatures ... cattle and creeping things and beasts of the earth."* And it was so. With a magnificent sense of humor, the Creator outdid Himself in the variety of animals He fashioned: the hippopotamus and giraffe, elephant and monkey, lion and snake—the world's first and greatest zoo, though without cages. The animals loved it!

CHAPTER SEVEN

*Then God said, "Let Us make man in Our image ..."*
*Genesis 1:26*

The Lord saved His biggest surprise for the end: the creation of humanity. Before this there had been only one intelligent being in the entire universe: God Himself. Now He graciously decided to create other intelligent beings as well, which is what the Book of Genesis means when it tells of God saying, *"Let Us make man in Our image."*

Humanity would be only a very dim reflection of the great Creator, of course, but now God could relate to the people He had created. He could speak to them and they would answer—something He could not do with plants and animals. In a sense, the Creator would now have company!

"God formed man ('Adam' in Hebrew) out of dust from the ground and breathed into his nostrils the breath of life, and he became a living being" the Bible tells us. God put Adam in charge of all of nature, even to the point of giving names to all the animals and birds that God had created.

Still, there was something missing. …

CHAPTER EIGHT

*The LORD God said, "It is not good for the man to be alone.
I will make a helper suitable for him." Genesis 2:18*

Was one man to enjoy God's Creation all by himself? After a short time, he would have become very, very lonely with no one to share his excitement at being alive and able to think and act and talk.

But the Lord had a marvelous solution, and some have called it God's greatest invention of all—the creation of woman. The Bible tells the colorful story:

*The LORD God caused the man to fall into a deep sleep; and while he was sleeping, He took one of the man's ribs and closed up the place with flesh. Then the LORD God made a woman from the rib He had taken out of the man, and He brought her to the man.* (Genesis 2:21–22)

Adam was totally delighted! Now he had *some* kind of helper indeed! More than that, he also had a companion, someone with whom to share the great adventure of life itself, someone to love and marry—a wife and a family to come. God was so good!

The joy of love between man and woman—with children as the wonderful result—is one of the great proofs that God exists. Who else could have thought up this marvelous arrangement?

CHAPTER NINE

*Thus the heavens and the earth were completed. … So on the seventh day [… God] rested from all the work of creating that He had done.*
*Genesis 2:1–2*

God, of course, did not *have* to rest as if He had exhausted Himself and needed some time off for relaxation. He could have gone on to create another universe on that seventh day had He chosen to do so! The Bible simply tells us here that our marvelously balanced universe was now complete. The Creator also set a perfect example, that all of us—men, women, and children—should set aside time for rest and relaxation. To make sure we remember that, He gave us a weekly reminder that the Sabbath is a day of rest. In biblical times, His people observed it on Saturday, while Christians switched to Sunday to honor Jesus' resurrection.

God had given man and woman a beautiful paradise in which to live. It was called the Garden of Eden, a perfect park in which everything was good and nothing went wrong. But *could* anything go wrong? Today, whenever a new product is manufactured, it's immediately tested. On a much higher level, God did the same thing. In the center of His lush garden, He fashioned what might be called a "test tree." God called it the Tree of the Knowledge of Good and Evil, and He warned Adam that this was the one tree whose fruit he should not eat or he would die. All the rest he could enjoy.

Now the big test: would human beings obey God?

CHAPTER TEN

*When the woman saw that the fruit of the tree was good for
food and pleasing to the eye, and also desirable for gaining
wisdom, she took some fruit and ate it. She also gave some
to her husband, who was with her, and he ate it. Genesis 3:6*

They failed the test!! It was a miserable, terrible failure!

Why didn't they obey God? Satan, in the form of a wily serpent, told the woman, Eve, that she would become like God Himself if she ate the fruit. So she did. Adam was no better and did the same. This was the first awful decision of humanity, which has been making bad decisions ever since. We call it "sin." Evil now entered the perfect world and caused a fracture between God and His creation.

God had warned that eating the forbidden fruit would bring death, but it didn't happen immediately. Suddenly, Adam and Eve noticed that something was wrong. Their beautiful bodies God had created were now something to be ashamed of, since they were naked. Having no clothes hadn't bothered them at all before this, but now they were embarrassed. They took the large leaves of a fig tree and sewed them together for clothing. Perhaps they hoped God wouldn't notice? Or should they try to hide from Him?

CHAPTER ELEVEN

*But the L*ORD *God called to the man, "Where are you?"*
*Genesis 3:9*

Adam and Eve couldn't hide from God, nor can any man, woman, or child since then. "I heard You in the garden," Adam replied, "and I was afraid because I was naked, and I hid myself."

"Who told you that you were naked?" asked God. "Have you eaten of the tree of which I commanded you not to eat?"

Adam admitted that he had, but … he selfishly shoved the blame onto his wife. He even blamed God. "The woman that You gave me," he said, "she made me eat." This man was no hero.

God now turned to the woman, but she blamed the serpent. Then God cursed the serpent. Adam and Eve's perfect life in paradise was ruined. Women would now have much pain at childbirth. Men would have to earn their food "by the sweat of their brow," and even the ground was now cursed with thorns, thistles, and ugly weeds. And yes, both husband and wife would now have to die, as have all their descendents ever since. Oh, and they were also expelled from the Garden of Eden, an undiscovered place that was now guarded by an angel with a flaming sword.

So, does the story end in disaster? Was Creation God's big mistake?

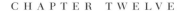

CHAPTER TWELVE

*[God said to the serpent,] "He will crush your head, and you will strike His heel." Genesis 3:15*

If Creation was a failure, why didn't the Creator simply uncreate everything?

Going back to a great black void was not in God's plans. He would fix it. Just as He brought order out of chaos, so He would now bring triumph out of tragedy.

God's words to the serpent are the very first announcement of a Savior to come. The offspring of Eve mentioned in Genesis 3:15 is Jesus. He would crush the head of Satan at the crucifixion. This would "strike His heel," to be sure, but God would finally conquer Satan and forgive human disobedience through Christ's death on Good Friday and resurrection on Easter. A very, very happy ending, indeed!

Science often tells the story of our beginnings a bit differently. In its "Big Bang" theory, a tiny cosmic egg the size of a marble exploded into the universe in one trillionth of a second. That's harder to believe than the Bible, yet it amounts to the same thing: God's instant creation. Science tells us that matter and energy are the two great building blocks of nature. So does the Bible. Science requires light before vegetation. So does the Bible. The various stages of a developing nature involving creatures in the sea and sky before mammals on land runs parallel in both the Bible and science. In fact, science gives us even more amazing detail about the immensity of the universe and our planet Earth, which can support life only because of a bewildering number of factors that had to be just right or life could never have happened—showing a divine design and intelligence behind it all.

This, then, is the magnificent story of how we all came to be. None of it was accidental. All of it is the Creator's great plan. Only God could have accomplished all this!